To Luke
on his fifth birthday
Love,
    Mom & Dad
        20 April 86

How Come...?
Easy Answers to Hard Questions

By Joyce Richards.

Illustrations by Susan Perl

Revised Edition

Platt & Munk, Publishers/New York
A Division of Grosset & Dunlap

This book is created from the award-winning advertising campaign for Health-tex clothes in response to requests from parents and educators all over the country.

1986 Printing

Copyright © 1975 by Health-tex, Inc., manufacturers of children's clothing. All rights reserved. No part of this book may be reproduced in any form without the express permission of the publishers. Printed in the United States of America. Published simultaneously in Canada.
Library of Congress Card Catalog No. 74–25004
ISBN 0-448-47484-0

Contents

Who thought up spaghetti?

We think the famous Italian explorer, Marco Polo, discovered spaghetti. He found the long, squiggly food in China and brought it back to Italy. The king named it spaghetti. And now spaghetti eaters are everywhere because nothing's more fun to eat than funny, skinny, scooting spaghetti. Put sauce on it, catch a piece and slide it down—ffloop!

Why is the ocean salty?

We believe the ocean gets its salt from the earth. Rocks have salt in them. Plants have salt in them. And there is salt in the soil. The rain falls and washes the salt out of the soil and into the sea. Rivers wear down the stones and carry more salt into the sea. You don't taste the salt in rivers because it doesn't have a chance to collect in them. You do taste it in the ocean because the ocean has been collecting salt for millions of years.

Why do birds sing?

Some people think birds sing just to make pretty music. But singing is a way some birds communicate with each other. Birds sing to warn strange birds to stay away from their nests or territory. Sometimes they sing to attract mates or to comfort their mates while the baby birds are hatching.

Some birds are very famous singers, like the wood thrush, nightingale, robin and the little pet canary. But not all birds sing. Some make other sounds to communicate, like owls that go "hoot, hoot" in the night.

People who like to hear birds sing often build little houses and put out food so the birds will come and stay.

What is a falling star?

When we see bright lights moving through the night sky, we say they are falling or shooting stars.

But they aren't really stars at all. A star is a heavenly body that shines by its own light. A falling star is really a small, stony mass we call a meteor.

We cannot see meteors until they enter the earth's atmosphere. Then, friction makes them so hot, they glow with a beautiful, fiery light until they fall to the ground and burn out.

Children all around the world think falling stars are lucky, so that when they see one, they make a wish on it.

Why do we eat turkey

The reason we eat turkey on Thanksgiving is to remind us of the Pilgrims who ate wild turkey on the first Thanksgiving in America. The reason the Pilgrims ate turkey was because it tasted good and was plentiful enough so everyone could have seconds.

When the first Pilgrims landed in Plymouth in 1620 they faced a very cold winter with very little food.

But then spring came and their Indian friend, Squanto, taught them how to fish and plant corn and hunt wild turkeys in the forest. They had plenty to eat. So when autumn came, the Pilgrims wanted to thank God for His goodness to them. They decided to have a feast and invite the Indians. On Thanksgiving day Chief Massasoit brought unexpected guests—90

on Thanksgiving?

braves. They sat down at long tables and ate for three days!

 Between courses the Pilgrim fathers and the Indians played games and ran races. The Pilgrim mothers and boys and girls cooked and cooked — Indian pudding, clam chowder, roasted corn, corn bread and nut stuffing for the big bird. The

Indians went home happy. And the Pilgrims stayed strong all winter in their 7 little houses. They had enough food in their 3 big storehouses to last until spring.

 Now we celebrate Thanksgiving on the fourth Thursday of November. And remember how many good things we have to be thankful for.

Why does a bee make honey?

A female bee makes honey in a special stomach that's like a little factory. But first she goes to a flower for the same reason you go to the supermarket. The flower contains the raw ingredients of honey.

She sips the sweet flower juice called <u>nectar</u> up through her mouth—which is shaped like a tiny soda straw—down into her honey stomach where it becomes the most healthful kind of sweet a person or a bee can eat.

If she ate all this honey herself, she'd get too fat to fly. So she wings back to the hive to feed the baby bees a delicious treat called bee bread made out of honey mixed with flower pollen.

BEE FARM

HONEY

Why are there zoos?

Zoos are for you so you can see and get to know animals you don't meet on every street corner. Peacocks not robins. Pandas not pussycats. Camels. Cougars.
Kangaroos. They all call zoos home when they aren't in their real homes in the wild.

And a good zoo is like home. It is airy and grassy with winds to cool off in. And zoo keepers serve just the kind of food each animal likes best.

A zoo protects the animals that are getting rare so they won't become extinct from enemies like forest fire and hunger and hunters.

And don't forget that animal animals are just like human animals. They do not like to be teased, or yelled at. When you go to the zoo it's important that you wear your best manners.

15

How many kinds of

Draft horse

There are five main kinds, and the work a horse does tells you what kind, or type, it is. The <u>draft horse</u> weighs nearly a ton and can haul heavy wagonloads. But once it was a war horse and carried a knight in armor and wore armor itself, over 400 pounds of it.

The <u>harness horse</u> is for high-stepping in front of a carriage. Before there were automobiles, people bought a 'heavy harness' breed if they needed something proud and dignified to drive. The creamy white Lippizaner was bred especially to draw the carriages of the Austrian Emperor. If he had wanted a sportier ride he would have driven a 'light harness' trotter or pacer.

Harness horse

horses are there?

Saddle horse

A <u>saddle horse</u> takes you riding or hunting. It is usually three-gaited. It will walk, trot, or canter when you tell it to.

A hunter is a horse that must jump, too, and have lots of stamina. Most hunters and race horses are Thoroughbreds which means they are descended from one of three famous sires brought to England in 1685.

A <u>stock horse</u> can stop, start and turn very quickly. It is the one work horse the truck and tractor can't replace.

The smallest and gentlest horse of all is the <u>pony</u>. If it is a Shetland, it may not be much taller than you are—from 38 to 46 inches.

Stock horse

No matter how big or little a horse is today, the first horse over 60,000,000 years ago was no bigger than a fox terrier. It lived in forests and browsed on leaves. It joined up with man right after the dog, the camel and the cow.

It is very fast. It had to be to outrun the wolves in those early days. It remembers everything. And it is rather timid. So when you go up to a horse, always remember to move and speak gently.

Where did the Easter bunny come from?

Long ago in Germany there was a folk tale about a bird who was turned into a rabbit. It was so happy with its new shape that it celebrated its first spring as a floppy-eared fluffy bunny by giving people gifts of something it knew how to make when it was a bird: eggs!

And to this day we love the idea of the bunny bringing eggs at Easter—chocolate and jelly eggs and colored real ones—to celebrate the re-birth of life in the growing-est season of all, the spring.

How do flies walk on the ceiling?

The plump little pads on all six of a fly's feet flatten out when it walks on a smooth surface and give off a sticky liquid that holds it to the wall or ceiling like glue. Fruit fly, frit fly, blue bottle, midge, mosquito, marsh fly, horse fly, house fly, gnat—all have funny fabulous feet. Squish-squish-squish-squish. That's a fly walking. Shoo!

How does a caterpillar

A caterpillar is a butterfly's baby and it grows in 3 stages—egg, caterpillar, chrysalis. The tiny egg is laid by its mother on a favorite leaf. Soon the tiny caterpillar inside chews through its shell and begins eating its leaf—and every other leaf around. It is very greedy.

It grows very fat, very fast. Its old skin gets too small and it has to wiggle out of it. A soft new skin is always ready underneath. This process is called molting. It molts 4 or 5 times in butterfly babyhood.

Sometimes it changes color and spots after a molt. But it keeps 6 real legs and all its soft baby legs to support its long back.

become a butterfly?

Then one day it loses its appetite and leaves its leaf. It goes looking up and down stems and stalks for a safe place to become a chrysalis. This will be its last molt. It gets a new skin and a new shape. It may look like a twig or a piece of bark. It stays quiet in its chrysalis for a long time.

Then one warm morning—pop!—the chrysalis cracks. And a gorgeous butterfly pokes out. Its wings are wet and rumpled at first. But soon it dries out and flutters off into the sun to mate with another butterfly. More eggs, caterpillars, chrysalids. The cycle never stops.

What are freckles?

Freckles are little brown spots that you can't wash off. Some people have them on their faces and other parts of their bodies.

Freckles are formed in the skin by a certain kind of coloring matter that we call <u>melanin</u>.

If your mother and father have freckles, you probably will, too. Sometimes you can get new ones by staying out in the sun, because the sun causes the melanin under your skin to make new freckles.

Why do we burp?

Maybe you ate or drank too much. Popcorn's burpy-making and so is soda pop. Or maybe you ate too fast and didn't chew every mouthful into tiny bits. Or maybe your belt's too tight. Then all of a sudden, sometimes before you can cover your mouth—b-u-r-p. Excuse me!

Babies burp after bottles. Everybody burps now and then. It's natural.

Why do we have belly buttons?

A belly button marks the spot in the center of your tummy where you were attached to your mother before you were born. You were linked to her—deep down in a special place inside her—by an <u>umbilical</u> cord. The cord worked like a kind of straw. For nine months food from your mother's body passed along the cord and into you so you could get big enough and strong enough to live by yourself in the world. Once you were here you didn't need the cord any more so the doctor tied it up and tucked it in. And there you have it still: a belly button, known in grown-up circles as a navel.

How did streets get their names?

Before streets had names, people had to say "Turn right at the old oak tree and follow the brook over the mountain." So they decided streets should have names. Guess what they named the road near the old oak. Oak Tree Road. By the brook? Brookside Way. On the mountain? Mountain Avenue.

Of course, some streets are called Avenues, Boulevards, Lanes and Ways. Usually, Avenues are big streets and Boulevards are even grander, while Lanes are little and winding, and Ways are even squigglier.

Of course, almost every town has a Main Street. It's usually the main or most important street. (Probably when the town was new, it was the *only* street!) Some streets, like Lee Avenue, are named for families who started the town. Others, like Roosevelt Avenue, for famous people. Others for what is—or used to be—on the street, like Windmill Road. What do you suppose is on School Street?

What good

Lots of insects, though not all of them, are very good. Bees, for instance, buzz-buzz-buzz from flower to flower, carrying the dusty yellow pollen plants need to make the seeds that make more plants. Without bees, we wouldn't have honey for our morning toast.

Silk worms are just as busy as bees. They spin fine, fine threads—some over 1000 feet long—that are used to weave soft, silk cloth.

Other insects are important because they hold bad bugs to a minimum. The skinny green praying mantis thinks pesty flies and mosquitoes are delicious. The plump red ladybug helps farmers protect their crops from another bad bug called an aphid. She has them for her dinner before they can chew up the food we need for our dinner.

Some insects are also fun to watch: butterflies, fireflies, and hard-working little ants.

27

How did sandwiches begin?

A long time ago in England there lived a man called the Earl of Sandwich. One day he was sitting at his table writing. He sat there a long time and he got very hungry, so he asked his servant to put a piece of meat between two slices of bread and bring it to him. No one had ever heard of doing such a thing before. But it was the servant's job to serve. So he gave the Earl exactly what he asked for: a piece of meat between two slices of bread. It must have tasted good because the next time he asked for a piece of cheese between the two slices of bread. And the time after that he asked for a piece of chicken between the slices of bread.

And before you could say peanut butter and jelly, everybody was eating this marvelous invention—even the servant. But no one knew what to call it. So they named it after the man who thought it up. And forever after two slices of bread with anything in the middle was called a sandwich.

Why does the moon shine?

 The moon is a huge ball of rock and dust and craters that has no light of its own. When we see it shining, we're really seeing the sun's light reflected on the moon. At very rare times the moon also shines by earthshine. Earthshine is light reflected on the moon by the earth.

Sometimes as it moves around the earth we see it as a big, round, gleaming silver balloon. Some nights it's just a thin squiggle of light. Sometimes it looks like it's only half there. But it always looks silvery bright when you stand in front of your house at night and look up at the sky.

And now that the astronauts have been to the moon, it's exciting to think that some day you might be able to go there, too.

What is a

COUSINS ARE ALSO FRIENDS

A relative is a member of your family. Your closest relatives are your mother and your father, your brothers and sisters. The next closest are your grandparents. They are your parents' parents. Your parents' brothers and sisters are your aunts and uncles. All their children are your cousins—which makes you a cousin too.

BABIES ARE NEW RELATIVES

Every time a relative has a baby you have a new playmate who is also a member of your family. Soon there are lots of young people who are your kinfolk.

relative?

Relatives keep adding up so quickly that the best way to keep track of them is on a family tree, with grandparents on the top and branches for everybody else to show exactly who is who.

How did Teddy bears get their name?

They were named after Theodore "Teddy" Roosevelt, our twenty-sixth President and a great outdoors man. One day in 1902 on a hunting trip in Mississippi, he heard a commotion in the underbrush: leaves trembled, twigs snapped. The bushes parted to reveal—an adorable, roly-poly baby bear.

The President refused to shoot, of course. The story was drawn up into a cartoon and got in all the newspapers. And soon everyone wanted a Teddy bear like Teddy's bear.

All Teddies look pretty much alike: button eyes, a cuddly body, a plushy coat the color of brown sugar. He may be tiny or tall. He may squeak when you hug him hard. Or just keep smiling. But he is always very strong because any Teddy worthy of his name will last as long as you need him.

Why do we have different color hair?

Red or blond, brown or black, or in-between, your hair is the color it is because of <u>genes</u>. Genes are tiny but important parts of your body that come to you from your mother and father. A gene from each of them combines to give you every physical characteristic you have, including hair color.

Sometimes one gene is <u>dominant</u>—or stronger. When that happens, your hair will be the color passed along by the stronger gene. If both parents have the same color hair, chances are you'll have it too.

A seed is a tiny package with the makings of a whole new plant inside it. It grows in the spring when the ground is warm and the rain and temperature are just right.

The spring rain drip-drip-drips down inside the seed coat. The sun shines. Soon the seed swells and pops open.

seeds grow?

Down go roots. Up shoots a leafy stem—right through the roof of earth. A plant is born.

Flowers and fruits and vegetables all grow from seeds and they make more seeds of their own. More daisies and buttercups, peas and limas, peanuts and pumpkins, apples and peaches, cucumbers and corn—there's no end to seeds.

35

Why do bees sting?

Nature gives creatures different ways to protect themselves and their homes. Nature gave some little bees a very sharp sting.

There are many different kinds of bees. Some don't sting at all. But bumblebees and honeybees are two of the ones that do. The bumblebee can sting over and over again. But the honeybee can sting only once, because its stinger is pulled out of its body when it stings.

Some people are afraid of bees because they sting. But since bees sting only when they're frightened or hurt, they usually won't hurt you if you don't bother them.

How many different kinds of colors are there?

Nobody ever counted exactly—but there are at least a million colors. (Look around you right now and you can count quite a few.)

No matter what color you see —purple or orange, pink or brown or green—it comes from mixing the three basic colors called the primary colors: blue, yellow and red.

Take some paint and try it yourself. Yellow + blue makes green. Red + yellow makes orange. Blue + red makes purple.

And all the colors smooshed together make—black.

What animals

There are over a million-and-a-half different kinds of animals in the world. But the ones whose birthdays are easiest to check are the vertebrates, or animals with backbones, like ourselves. A vertebrate can be a mammal (that's you), a bird, a fish, an amphibian (that's an animal that spends its life in and out of water), or a reptile.

Among <u>mammals</u>—and a mammal is usually an animal that has hair and nurses its young—man lives the longest: 113 years. Elephants come next with grandfathers of 70. A gorilla who takes care of itself can get to be 60. A lucky rhinoceros will reach 49. A horse is very old at 30.

<u>Birds</u> generally outlive mammals, parrots chat-

live the longest?

ting on till 100, eagles swooping and diving and seeing 80 anyway . . . 22-year-old canaries aren't unheard of.

A carp, 50. A halibut, 60. An aged beluga sturgeon that wins fins down at 70. How do we know? From growth rings on the fish scales and bones.

One famous pet toad lived with his adoptive family for 36 years. But another amphibian, the giant Japanese salamander, got to be bigger (5 feet long) and older (55).

Monster tortoises are related to dinosaurs and other more recent reptiles and live perhaps 200 years. But nobody knows for sure.

Why do we need vitamins?

If we want to have bright eyes and rosy cheeks, we need vitamin A.

If we want to have enough energy for work and play, we need the B vitamins.

If we don't want to get sick a lot, we need vitamin C.

If we want to have strong straight bones and teeth, we need vitamin D.

In fact, we need many different vitamins in order to live healthy, normal lives, because our bodies cannot get along without them.

Fortunately there are vitamins in almost everything we eat. To make sure we get all the vitamins we need, we should eat wholesome foods from each of these categories.

1) Milk, butter, eggs, and cheese.
2) Yellow and leafy green vegetables.
3) Meat, poultry, and fish.
4) Whole-grain breads and cereals.
5) Citrus and other fruits.

What is paper made of?

Most paper is made from trees cut down and sliced into tiny chips no bigger than postage stamps. The wood chips are cooked in a big vat with water and chemicals. The cooked mixture is called pulp and it looks like oatmeal.

When it's clean and de-lumped, it trickles through a long machine whose hot rollers squeeze the pulp flat and dry into a giant piece of paper 30 feet wide and hundreds of feet long.

Paper can be made from cotton fibers. Paper can also be made from paper itself. This is known as recycled paper and is very important to us, because then fewer new trees are cut down.

Do cats really have nine lives?

No, it just seems that way because a jump or fall that would hurt a person is nothing to a cat. It is so relaxed, rubbery and strong that it usually, though not always, lands on its feet. A cat can pussyfoot along spiky fences.

It can hear a mouse in its hole. It can see in the almost dark and guide itself by its whiskers. It can even retract its claws until it needs them.

A cat is clever, curious and no person is its master. Still, a cat truly loves its people family and is the only animal with a special way of telling them just how much, with its rickety-rackety purr.

Why am I ticklish?

Your skin is made up of millions of little receptors, or nerve endings, that tell you whether you're warm or cold or being touched by something. Some places are more sensitive than others because they have more receptors.

When something light and pleasant—like a feather or a blade of grass or a friend's tickling finger—touches your ticklish spot, all the little nerves in the vicinity tell the other nerves all along the line till your brain gets the message: kitchy-koo!

You can't help being ticklish any more than you can stop an itch or a sneeze.

So give in and giggle.

When you dress up like a goblin or ghost or witch or some strange, scary creature on Halloween, you are doing more than wearing a funny costume, you are following a tradition that has been going on in different ways for thousands of years.

The earliest we can trace it is back to the Druids, an order of priests who lived in ancient times in the lands that are now Britain, Ireland and France. They were very superstitious people who believed that on October 31st, all the wicked people who had died came back to earth, often in animal shapes. That's why we still see black cats, ghosts and cemeteries associated with Halloween.

lloween start?

Romans also had a festival about this time. Every year they held a great feast to celebrate the autumn harvest. That's why we still use colorful autumn foods such as pumpkins and apples as Halloween decorations.

The name Halloween started in the eighth century, when the Roman Catholic Church declared November 1st as All Saints Day. The day before was a hallowed evening, or Halloween. The ancient pagan customs were still so popular, they were combined into this Christian feast day.

Our Halloween of course is very different from the ancient ones. Today instead of frigntening people, it lets them have a lot of fun.